KITTEN

HOW TO USE THIS BOOK

Read the captions in the eight-page booklet and using the labels beside each sticker, choose the kitten that best fits in the space available.

•

Don't forget that your stickers can be stuck down and peeled off again. If you are careful, you can use your kitten stickers more than once.

•

You can also use your kitten stickers to make your own book, or for project work at school.

First Published in Great Britain in 1996
by Dorling Kindersley Limited,
A Penguin Company
80 Strand, London WC2R 0RL

Copyright © 1996 Dorling Kindersley Limited, London

Visit us on the World Wide Web at http://www.dk.com

Written and edited by Nicola Waine
Designed by Joseph Hoyle

ISBN 0-7513-5474-0

Reproduced by Colourscan, Singapore

Printed and bound in China by L.Rex Printing Co., Ltd.

A DORLING KINDERSLEY BOOK

Curious kittens

Play is a very important part of a kitten's development. If it has brothers and sisters to play with before it is seven weeks old, a kitten should grow into a confident and strong cat. Through games, kittens practise how to hide, fight, and hunt. Playing teaches them how other kittens will react to their movements, and helps them to form friendships with their owners.

Growing up
By the time a kitten is about seven weeks old, it can balance and walk like an adult, and it can hold and grip objects. This kitten is calmly investigating its toy, and will soon be able to hunt alone successfully.

Communal cleaning
Although cats are independent animals, they still enjoy sociable behaviour, particularly as kittens. Grooming is an important part of family life.

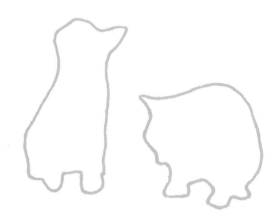

Object awareness
These kittens are becoming aware of objects around them. By watching the way things move, and by following the noises they make, kittens learn about the connections between sound and movement.

Early advantage
Kittens that don't have the chance to play during the early weeks of their lives are more likely to grow into unsociable, quiet cats. Those with brothers and sisters develop quickly and learn by watching and playing together.

Four in the bed
Kittens are most active early in the morning and late at night. They regularly doze during the day after energetic play. As they get older, the social bonds will break down and they will prefer to sleep alone.

Fearless friends
Most animals feel very exposed lying on their backs once they reach adulthood. Young kittens however don't feel such fear, and they enjoy the comfort and security of human contact.

Head-to-head
A cat shows friendship by rubbing its head against its owner or other animals. Kittens practise this in their play, and relaxed head-to-head contact is part of their development.

In training
This kitten is practising a "bird swat". It is too young now to reach properly, but soon it will leap into the air to catch its prey.

Gripping power
By eight weeks, kittens have full control over their paws, and can grip and carry things. Once they have learned to hold objects, they can become possessive like a small child and refuse to share their toys.

Mirror, mirror
Kittens have pupils that grow very large in the dark and very small in bright light, so that the eyes can always regulate the intake of light. Although they cannot see any better than humans, they are better at working in the dark.

Hide and seek
All kittens have a natural curiosity, and from three weeks, as their movements improve, they begin to explore. They will climb and hide inside things, learning about their surroundings and their own bodies.

Entertaining a friend
While a kitten is young, it is curious about other animals. The position it is sitting in indicates that it isn't scared, or a danger to the frog. Meeting other animals at this age means it will be well-socialized when older.

Starting to stalk
Kittens have developed hunting behaviour by about five weeks. They start to stalk each other at about three weeks, and chase objects soon after that.

Forever young
By keeping cats as pets, we ensure that they always have enough food, warmth, and companionship. They don't need to become independent as they would in the wild, and even when they are adult, they will happily play like kittens.

Body talk
Cats have very graceful and agile bodies. Their skeleton is designed to help them jump, pounce, and balance well. Kittens start to use their full range of movements when they are about four weeks old.

Full examination
This kitten is mimicking its mother's behaviour and smelling its "prey" before tasting it. The mother has taught her litter to investigate things through smell, touch, and taste.

Various breeds

There are many types of kittens, of various colours, sizes, and lengths of fur. Some kittens look completely different from their parents. There are over 100 pedigree breeds, and many more non-pedigree types, produced by parents of different breeds. Kittens inherit characteristics of both parents, so each one in a litter may be slightly different.

Mix and match
This kitten had a Blue-cream Shorthair mother, and a Blue Shorthair father. Its brothers and sisters could be either pure cream, or blue, or a mix.

Points of colour
This is a colour-point kitten, which means that it has areas of darker fur on its face, ears, legs, feet, and tail. The points can be many different colours, from brown and silver to blue.

Show kitten
These are friendly Brown Classic Tabby kittens. If this breed is entered in a show, the cats must have orange eyes and a brick-red nose.

A unique pet
These kittens are cross-breed kittens, their parents were different breeds of cat. Non-pedigree kittens inherit characteristics from their pedigree parents, so a long-haired cross-breed may behave like a long-haired pedigree.

Gentle red-head
The Red Tabby is friendly and gentle, like most long-haired kittens. Its hair is silky and fine, and needs regular grooming.

Elegant Asian
This tiny kitten is a Singapura, bred from the feral cats of Singapore. The kitten's coat gets shorter in appearance as it gets older, and its eyes change from green to blue.

Dual nationality
This kitten is an Asian Red Cornelian, although the breed was developed in Britain. They are lively, friendly kittens with fine, short hair.

Oriental family
These are Oriental Chocolate Spotted kittens, with their grandfather. They are lively pets, descended from Siamese cats. The kittens have a solid line down their spines, but this should become spotted as they grow.

COLOURS AND MARKINGS

A curious
ginger kitten

A rare white
tiger cub

A playful
tortoiseshell

A patchy tortie and
white kitten

Unusual
Chocolate
and Lilac
Shorthairs

A distinctive,
spotted Bengal
Leopard

A Blue and White
British Shorthair

A Cinnamon Angora
with her three kittens

A Blue-grey
Chartreux

A Blue Spotted
British
Shorthair

A pale Birman kitten
with her mother

A Birman
kitten with a
black-tipped
Burmilla

Creamy
Siamese
kittens

A blue and
cream cross-breed

A timid
Chocolate
Shorthair

LONG-HAIRED

Long-haired Birman kittens

A ginger kitten
learning to socialize

Brown Classic Tabby kittens

A beautiful, thick coated Silver
Tabby and her kitten

A young
Silver Tabby

A Ragdoll charmer

A Red Tabby

A litter of curious
Birman kittens

A Silver Shaded
Persian kitten

A Persian hunter

Tabby and ginger
cross-breeds

A blue-eyed
Cinnamon Angora

A Birman baby

A Blue-cream Persian

Blue and white
cross-breed kittens

SHORT-HAIRED

A hungry
cream tabby

An elegant
Singapura
kitten

A cat-napping
tortoiseshell

Cross-breed kittens
playing hide and seek

A tiny brown
tabby

A blue and
cream cross-
breed kitten

A playful
Oriental kitten

A young
puma cub

A cream colour-point
kitten

Blue and Cream British
Shorthairs

A domestic
relative of
the African
wild cat

A balancing
tortoiseshell

A ginger with an
unusual friend

A curious
Red Cornelian

A flexible
Siamese kitten

KINDS OF KITTENS

A five-week-old
tabby kitten

A tabby nursing
her litter

Shorthaired
Oriental
kittens

A playful
tortie tabby

A Siamese kitten
with its mother

Newborn kittens
huddling together

Tabby and tortoiseshell
kittens

A prowling tiger cub

A contented
patched tabby
kitten

A wide-eyed
young cream
kitten

A Blue-cream
Persian

A basket of
sleepy tabbies

A watchful
leopard cub

Birman
playmates

A six-day-old tabby
snuggling its mother

Dark chocolate
Chocolate Shorthairs are not very common, but they are calm, friendly cats who make excellent pets. While they are kittens, the tabby markings are still quite clear.

Clever camouflage
There are many different types of tabby pattern, found on both domestic pets and wild cats. The spots and stripes provide excellent camouflage and help them hide and hunt more effectively.

Birman legend
The original Birman is said to have been a white temple cat. It sat with the head priest as he lay dying, and where it touched him with its paws and face, the cats fur turned a darker shade.

Floppy kittens
Ragdoll kittens make ideal family pets. They become very limp and relaxed when they are picked up, which is how they got their name, and they love being stroked and fussed over.

Shining example
While young, Silver Tabby kittens are often mainly black, with just traces of silver. They are among the most beautiful cats when fully grown with silver coats.

Playful Angora
Litters of the Cinnamon Angora rarely have less than three kittens. They have long triangular heads, sharp ears, and fine, silky fur. These kittens are friendly and playful, and make lively pets.

French pedigree
This sturdy kitten is a Blue-grey Chartreux. Legend says that this friendly French breed was developed by monks in a monastery near Grenoble in the 1300s.

"Spotties"
Cats with spotted markings date back as far as Ancient Egypt. This is the Blue Spotted British Shorthair. Although the spots aren't all the same size, they are quite clearly defined.

Colour confusion
This Silver Shaded Persian kitten looks like a Chinchilla kitten. In fact, if these kittens become paler in colour as they grow, they are often then called Chinchillas.

Kitten care

Kittens are blind and helpless for their first nine days, and they usually stay with their mother to be fed and protected until they are about nine weeks old. A kitten will learn to groom and ask for food by watching its mother. Once they are old enough, kittens are happy to live with human families.

Man handled
Kittens do not always enjoy being picked up. They need to feel relaxed and secure, so cradle them carefully.

Sibling rivalry
The constant rivalry for food and attention in a large litter means that the kittens tend to be alert and active. They should grow into playful, curious, and lively cats.

Top to tail
Kittens learn how to wash themselves by watching their mother. They are naturally very clean animals, and grooming is instinctive when a kitten is relaxed.

Basic training
Litter training is one of the first things you must do with a new kitten. Cats are fussy about smells and texture, so once they are happy using a litter tray, it is best not to change the type of litter you use.

Scratch and sniff
Smell and taste are important senses for a young kitten. Smell is the first to develop, and the most useful when investigating its surroundings.

Well groomed
Long-haired kittens need regular grooming to prevent their coats becoming matted. Most cats enjoy being brushed; it feels similar to their mother licking their fur.

Family connections
As a kitten's senses develop, it learns the scent of its mother and associates it with comfort and security. It will keep coming back to her for protection as it starts to explore.

Powers of concentration
These kittens are focusing on a toy. They have learned that if they look away, it may move. This is instinctive hunting behaviour, which is often shown in play.

Wash with mother

Being groomed by its mother not only teaches a kitten how to keep itself clean, it also strengthens the bond between the mother and the kitten. Kittens begin to clean each other as they get older for the same reason.

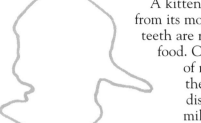

Milk teeth

A kitten stops feeding from its mother when its teeth are ready for solid food. Cats get plenty of moisture from their food, but a dish of water, or milk for younger kittens, is also necessary.

Comfort food

These kittens don't need their mother's milk any more, but feel comforted by staying close to her, as though they were still feeding.

Touching behaviour

Stroking your kitten every day ensures that it will grow up enjoying the company of humans. It also helps the kitten feel secure without its mother.

Central heating

These kittens are huddled together to keep warm while their mother looks for food.

Young developer

At just three weeks, a kitten can support its body and walk, although its balance is poor. By the time it is five weeks old, all its senses and its balance are fully developed.

Professional sleepers

Kittens will always look for warm, secure places to sleep. They sleep for about 16 hours a day, almost twice as long as most other mammals.

Natural carers

Fostering is a natural instinct in cats, developed so that one mother could go and hunt while another would nurse the litters. Cats will happily accept orphaned kittens if they have just given birth.

Early learning

Kittens develop curiosity earlier than fear, so a mother's role includes keeping them out of trouble. Until they are about six weeks old, she is their main source of emotional and physical development.

Wild kittens

There are wild cats all over the world. They are not pack animals, and usually like to live alone once they are adult. Wild kittens, or cubs, have to grow up quickly and learn to defend themselves and hunt for food. Cubs often have fur which provides camouflage, to protect them while young, and then help them hide when they hunt. All domestic kittens are descended from small wild cats such as the African wild cat, and there is even evidence that cavemen kept pet cats.

White beauty

The striking white tiger was once a familiar sight in north and east India. There are now only a few left. The colour comes from a white gene similar to that found in domestic cats. Tiger cubs have very large feet and look quite clumsy until their bodies catch up.

Under threat

Leopard cubs are cared for by their mother until they are about two years old. They are skilled climbers, and often carry their prey into a tree for safety before eating it. The number of leopards is decreasing rapidly. Humans hunt them for their fur, and are also destroying their natural habitat.

Spots and stripes

The puma is very like a domestic cat, and even purrs like one. Although the cub is marked with spots, these will soon merge to become the stripes of an adult puma.

Burning bright

The tiger is the largest and most powerful of all cats. They need a great deal of meat to survive, so they are skilled hunters and work at night. The tiger is an endangered species, and cubs are especially vulnerable until they are independent.

A friendly wild cat

This non-pedigree blue and white kitten is directly related to the African wild cat. The Victorians used cats like this to breed the British Shorthair. When breeding pedigree cats from cross-breeds, the cats are chosen for certain qualities, such as their colour or temperament.

Asian hunter

The Bengal Leopard is a domestic pet, developed from the Asian leopard. Its coat is very distinctive, and looks similar to a leopard's. This kitten is friendly and gentle, and the fur is now the only thing that betrays its wild ancestry.